Digging
For
Dinos

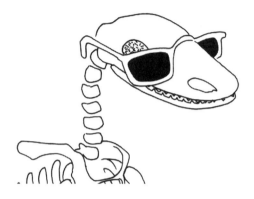

This book is fiction. The people, places, events, and eyeglass wearing dinosaurs depicted within are fictitious. Any resemblance to persons living or dead or to real life places is purely coincidence and, in all honesty, probably a little disturbing.

ISBN 978-0-9785642-1-6

Printed in the U.S.A.

First Printing, April 2008

Beaches, Bones, and Petoskey Stones ...

Who Knows What Dinosaurs Are Made Of?

CONTENTS

Real Heroes Read!

realheroesread.com

#4: Digging For Dinos

David Anthony

and

Charles David

Illustrations

Lys Blakeslee

Traverse City, MI

Home of the Heroes

abigail

zoë

andrew

CHAPTER 1:
MEET THE HEROES

Welcome to Traverse City, Michigan, population 18,000. The city has everything you might expect: malls, movie theaters, schools, and playgrounds. Kids swim here in the summer and build snowmen during the winter. Sometimes they pretend that they live in an ordinary place.

But Traverse City is far from ordinary. It is set on one of the Great Lakes and its beaches are crowded most every summer day. Thousands of people visit every year.

Still, few of them know the city's real secret. Even fewer talk about it. You see, Traverse City is home to three daring superheroes. This story is about them.

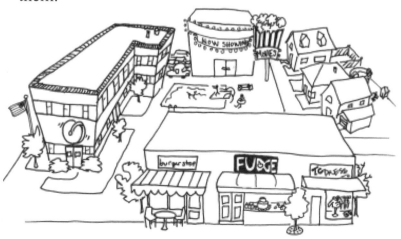

Meet Abigail, the oldest of our heroes by a whole eight minutes. When it comes to sports, she can't be beat—not at dunking, not at diving, and certainly not at dodge ball. Sometimes she's even called on to make the big rescues on Grand Traverse Bay. No one is a better swimmer or lifeguard.

Andrew comes next. He's Abigail's twin brother, younger by a measly eight minutes. If it has wheels, Andrew can ride it. We're talking anything with wheels, no matter how many. From unicycles to 18-wheelers, he is dazzling, daring, and dynamite on wheels.

Last but definitely not least is Baby Zoë. She's
proof that big things can come in small packages.
She still wears a diaper, but her breath is as strong as
a hurricane. Zoë puts the *pow* in power.

Together these three heroes keep the streets and neighborhoods of Traverse City and Michigan safe. Together they are …

CHAPTER 2:
SANDWICHES

"Is that all you've got?" Abigail challenged her brother. "Pick up the pace, Wheelie-boy!"

"Double-time!" Zoë ordered.

Ahead of them, Andrew smiled to himself and pedaled harder. He was already racing faster than the proverbial speeding bullet. Now it was time to kick his superpowers into high gear.

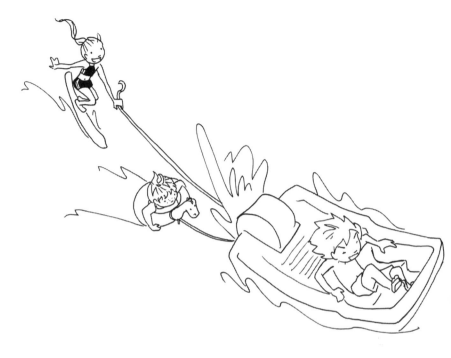

"Hold onto your hot rods!" he shouted over his shoulder.

He was spending a perfect summer day at the beach with his family. Perfect for him because he got to go fast. Perfect for his sisters because they got to tag along for the ride.

Not that Andrew minded. He lived for speed. Today that meant he was pedaling a paddleboat and towing his sisters behind him. Abigail was water-skiing on the left—slalom-style, the showoff. Zoë squealed and whooped from her seat on an inner tube.

Only one thing could interrupt their fun.

"Lunchtime!"

That was it. A call from Mom. It was as powerful a summons as Batman's Bat-Signal. When the heroes heard it, they responded immediately and without exception. They zoomed over to Mom on the double.

That was her superpower, making them hurry. The heroes knew who was the boss of them.

When they got to shore, Dad met them with a grin. "Why doesn't anyone go hungry at the beach?" he asked.

Abigail and Andrew groaned. "Because of all the sand which is there," they said in unison, sounding like bored robots.

Sand which is. Get it? *Sandwiches.* Dad asked the same old joke on every visit to the beach.

"Duh," Zoë muttered, crossing her eyes.

Still, everyone laughed. Being together as a family sometimes made bad jokes funny. Especially if lunch was on the way.

Mom raised a tray piled high with sand-wiches. "Who's ready to eat?" she asked. "I made everyone's favorite."

Everyone's favorite indeed, but not what you might expect. There was no boring bologna. No plain PB&J. Mom made super-sandwiches for super-hungry heroes.

"Dig in!" Dad urged, and he couldn't have been more right. Little did he know that soon the heroes would be doing exactly that. But not for sandwiches. They would be digging for dinos.

CHAPTER 3:
DIGGING FOR DINOS

When the heroes finished eating, they shared a quick look. They didn't need to say a word. All three of them were thinking the same thing, and the look confirmed it.

Time to hit the waves.

"Thanks for lunch, Mom," Abigail said.

"Thanks, Dad," Andrew added.

"Danke," Zoë shouted, halfway to the lake.

Mom stopped them with a single word. "Halt!" Her voice sounded like a knight's whose job it is to guard the castle gate.

"You just ate," she explained. "No swimming for fifteen minutes."

As one, the heroes groaned. They knew the stories and the rule. Swimming too soon after eating could be trouble. A cramp could strike and drag you deep beneath the waves.

Just exactly what a cramp was, Zoë didn't know. It sounded like some kind of creepy fish-monster to her.

There was no point in arguing. Mom never budged. The heroes wouldn't be allowed to dip even a big toe in the water for fifteen minutes no matter what.

Andrew slumped onto the sand, feeling sorry for himself. "Now what do we do?" he whined. "Fifteen minutes is *forever.*"

"We can bury you in the sand," Abigail suggested, teasing only a little. Oh, the fun she would have seeing her brother helpless and buried up to his neck!

Thankfully for Andrew, Zoë had a different idea. One that didn't involve burying him, at least not directly.

"Dig!" she exclaimed. "Dinos!"

Abigail and Andrew looked at each other, trying not to laugh. Dig for dinosaurs? What a ridiculous idea! Everyone knew that dinosaur bones weren't buried in the sand around Lake Michigan.

Not that playing along would hurt. It could even be fun. Lots of things ended up lost in the sand—spare change, jewelry, Petoskey stones, keys. Who knew what the heroes would find?

To no one's surprise, Zoë didn't wait. She had already decided that digging was a good idea. Talking about it wouldn't make her and her siblings famous archaeologists. Digging for dinos would.

So she jumped in with both hands. Yes, her hands, not her feet. Most people jumped in the other way around, but Zoë had a plan. She floated upside down, summoned her super-speed, and started digging.

Andrew and Abigail had little choice but to help. Zoë already had quite a hole started, and it was dig or get buried. Some choice. Neither of them liked getting sand in their swimsuits.

"After you," Andrew smiled, pretending to be polite. He really didn't want to be the first into the hole Zoë was digging.

"No, no," Abigail smiled back. "After you. I insist."

With that, she pushed him into the hole.

CHAPTER 4:
JUST HOW DEEP

"Oh, no, you don't!" Andrew howled as he started to fall into the sandy hole.

Maybe he wasn't as strong as Zoë. Maybe he wasn't as fast as Abigail—not without wheels, anyhow. But he was still strong and fast enough to do what needed to be done.

Smack!

With a slap of skin on skin, he snatched Abigail's ankle and yanked her into the hole with him. Together they tumbled into darkness.

Down and down and down they fell.

Just how deep did Zoë dig? Abigail wondered as her arms and legs whirled.

Wind howled in her ears, and the light above faded fast. Dark shapes whipped past her on both sides, always too quickly to be clearly seen.

Was that a pirate's buried treasure? An ant colony shaped like Joe Louis Arena? Maybe their neighbor Mrs. Diana Might* mining?

Abigail just couldn't be sure of anything in the dark.

* See Heroes A2Z #2: Bowling Over Halloween.

Andrew, however, saw none of those things. His imagination took over instead. He wasn't falling farther and farther into the earth. He imagined that he was floating free like an astronaut drifting through deep space.

Until he crashed into a passing comet, that is. Only the passing comet wasn't passing, and its name was Zoë.

THUMP!

And she had a friend named Abigail.

THUMP!

In other words, Andrew's fall ended when he landed on Zoë and Abigail landed on him. It was a one-two punch with a knockout in between.

"Deflated," Zoë gasped from the bottom of the pile. With her bigger siblings on top of her, she felt like a flattened balloon.

"Oops, sorry," Abigail apologized as she climbed awkwardly to her feet.

"Yeah, Zoë, sorry," echoed Andrew. "But why did you dig so deep?"

Zoë didn't waste time trying to catch her breath before explaining.

"Drawings," she said, pointing excitedly.

Ahead of her stretched a long underground tunnel. It was empty and unremarkable except for on thing. Dozens of cave paintings covered its walls.

The paintings, however, weren't like any the heroes had seen before. They didn't show antelopes or buffaloes or hunters on the prowl.

These paintings depicted dinosaurs, including a smallish one wearing eyeglasses!

CHAPTER 5:
JURASSIC ELEMENTARY

"Home run!" Abigail gasped in surprise.

"Off road," Andrew gawked.

Only Zoë didn't speak. She smiled, crossed her arms, and gave her siblings an I-told-you-so look. She had known that they could dig up some dinos, and the cave paintings proved it. Dozens of different dinosaurs were pictured, not only the one in glasses. The heroes were definitely on the right track.

"Why would a dinosaur wear eyeglasses?" Abigail wondered aloud. That confused and surprised all of them. None of the other dinosaurs in the paintings wore glasses.

And there were a lot to choose from—painting after painting after painting. They depicted dinosaurs playing, dinosaurs exercising, dinosaurs dancing, sitting, and sleeping. Every kind of dinosaur doing every kind of thing.

But only one of the dinosaurs wore glasses. They made that one dino look like some kind of prehistoric teacher.

"Let's see where this tunnel goes," Andrew suggested. His love for wheels always kept him on the move. He couldn't sit still for long.

So the heroes tiptoed to the end of the tunnel. They passed even more cave paintings along the way, all of which included the dinosaur with glasses.

A sign overhead finally caused them to stop. It was chiseled into the rock above an open doorway and looked like something out of the Flintstones.

In block letters it read, "Jurassic Elementary."

    A cave as big as a school classroom opened
beyond the doorway beneath the sign. Bulky desks
and chairs carved out of rock sat in neat rows facing
the same direction. A larger desk at one end faced
all of the others.

    The cave wasn't just the size of a classroom.
It *was* a classroom.

"Do you think the dinosaur with the glasses was the teacher?" Abigail asked. Every classroom needed a teacher.

"Let's find out," Andrew smirked. He was leaning against the far wall in know-it-all fashion. He had one arm draped over a lumpy design sticking out of the wall.

At first the design looked like nothing out of the ordinary. Just a natural formation in the rock. But a second glance revealed more.

The design was actually a cluster of fossils trapped in the wall. The heroes had really found a dinosaur!

CHAPTER 6:
THE MISSING PIECE

A real dinosaur! What were the odds of finding one in Traverse City? But the heroes had done exactly that, and they weren't finished.

"Duck!" Zoë warned, waving for her siblings to get out of the way. Then she squinted her eyes and lasers sprang from them toward the fossils in the wall.

Pew! Pew! Pew!

Like a jeweler cutting the perfect diamond, Zoë carefully sliced through the rock. Pebbles and dust fell away from her incisions, but not even the smallest fragment of fossil was harmed.

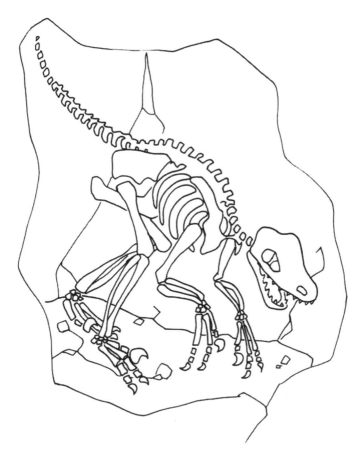

When Zoë finally closed her eyes, the heroes held their breath. They watched in anxious silence as the dust slowly settled and an unbelievable sight took shape.

The dinosaur was free! Zoë had done it. The fossils made up a complete skeleton that was now standing in a hollowed-out cubby that was like a tiny closet.

"Touchdown!" Abigail cheered her sister. "That's the way to cut through the defense."

Andrew couldn't agree more. Zoë was amazing. The dinosaur skeleton was in perfect shape. Imagine if it were more than just bones!

Zoë, however, wasn't impressed. She studied the skeleton like an artist inspecting her work for imperfections.

"Deficient," she said at last, frowning the slightest bit.

Deficient? The twins knew what that meant. Zoë thought the skeleton was incomplete, like a puzzle with a missing piece. And she wouldn't be happy until she found it.

Luckily Zoë had a simple solution. Petoskey stones. They were the official state stone and found only on the shores of northwestern Michigan. The stones were made of fossilized coral and left behind by glaciers. Tourists and local residents alike enjoyed searching for them on beaches, polishing them in rock tumblers, and using them to make jewelry.

From her superhero's cape, Zoë pulled two Petoskey stones. They were the size of chicken eggs and polished so that they glistened as if wet.

Next she flew over to the skeleton, curtseyed politely in the air, and then gently placed the stones in the dinosaur's eye sockets.

What happened next happens only to super-heroes. The skeleton coughed, shook itself like a wet dog, and came to life. Then it spoke.

"Oh, dear. I seem to have misplaced my glasses."

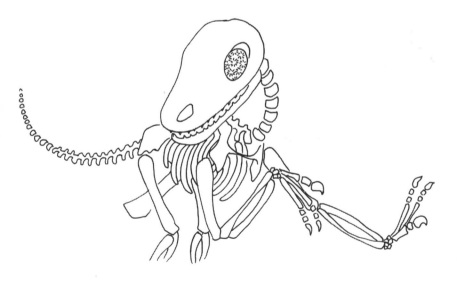

CHAPTER 7:
PROFESSOR B.C.

"*H*-here," Abigail stammered. "You can have *m*-mine."

Without really thinking about it, she handed her sunglasses to the dinosaur. Make that the *talking* dinosaur. Who wouldn't give a talking dinosaur their sunglasses when it asked for them? Who wouldn't give it *anything* it wanted?

The dinosaur accepted the sunglasses and put them on. Instantly it looked more comfortable. More like it did in the cave paintings.

"Excellent," it said with a bow. "Please accept my gratitude. I humbly thank you."

The heroes said nothing in response. They just stared with their mouths open. Finding a dinosaur was unbelievable. Finding one that talked was impossible. Or so they had thought.

"Forgive me," the dinosaur went on. "Let me introduce myself. I am Professor Brian Cranium. Professor B.C. for short. I am a smartasaurus. Maybe you have heard of me?"

The heroes shook their heads. No, they had never heard of a smartasaurus before, especially not one named Professor B.C.

Andrew shrugged. "I'm Andrew," he said slowly. "And these are my sisters, Abigail and Zoë. Together we are—"

"Heroes!" Professor B.C. applauded, cutting him off. "I see. Of course, of course. Zoë, Abigail, and Andrew. $H = ZA^2$. How nice to meet you."

"It's a pleasure to meet you, too," Abigail finally said.

"Delightful," Zoë agreed.

The girls decided that if Andrew could talk to the dinosaur, so could they. Their Dad, however, had other plans.

"Abigail, Zoë, Andrew!" he called from the beach far above. "Time to go home. Let's move!"

"Will you be here tomorrow?" Andrew asked as he turned to leave.

The heroes hated to go, and couldn't take Professor B.C. with them. The dinosaur wasn't a stray kitten they had found wandering in the street. Mom would never let them keep it.

"With pleasure," Professor B.C. told Andrew. "Now hurry home. Your family is waiting."

So the heroes sped back through Zoë's tunnel and up to the beach.

"Took you long enough" Dad winked when he saw them. "Did you dig all the way to China?"

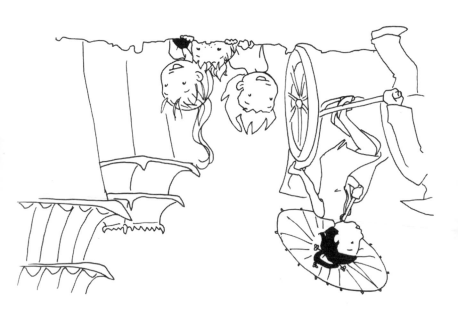

That night the heroes slept badly. They were too excited and too busy imagining the fun they would have with their very own dinosaur.

Abigail decided that she and Professor B.C. could show-off at Legion Park. No dog and owner would be able to match their tricks.

Andrew thought he would teach the dinosaur about wheels and everything that can be done with them. From cars to carriages and skates to scooters, he would leave nothing out.

Of course he would start off easy. A bicycle would do just fine.

Zoë just wanted another playmate. Nothing fancy. She didn't need to show off or use her superpowers. She and Professor B.C. could have tea parties in the backyard.

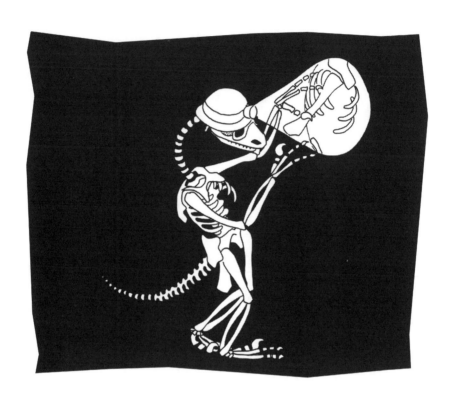

Even Professor B.C. had his own plans. While the heroes lay restlessly in bed, he was working. In fact, he worked all evening and all through the night. The moon came and went, but he did not stop to rest once.

There was too much to do. Too many of his friends to awaken.

Superhero kids, you see, were not the only ones who could dig for dinos.

CHAPTER 8:
DINOSAUR-SIZED HELP

The next morning, the heroes woke early, dressed fast, and tiptoed quietly out of the house. Their plan was simple. Find Professor B.C. and let the fun begin.

Unfortunately for them, not all plans go according to plan.

They got to the beach late. Long after most everyone else. Their neighbors were already there. Their friends were already standing in the crowd. Even the police were on the scene. Lots and lots of police.

"What's going on?" Abigail wondered. Professor B.C. was supposed to be their secret. "Did you guys tell someone?" she asked her siblings.

Zoë and Andrew shook their heads. They hadn't said anything to anyone.

Suddenly the crowd parted as if an elephant were charging through. Professor B.C. appeared in the vacated space carrying a bullhorn.

"Good morning, Traverse City!" he shouted cheerfully into the horn.

The crowd fell silent. No one knew what to expect. Most of them had never seen a walking, talking dinosaur skeleton before.

"Good morning," Professor B.C. repeated. "Good morning and hello. My friends and I are here to help."

Abigail shot her brother a look. *Friends?* she mouthed silently.

"The special power of your state's Petoskey stones has awakened us," the smartasaurus continued. "Now see what our power can do for you!"

"Tyrannosaurus Rex is strong and never tires."

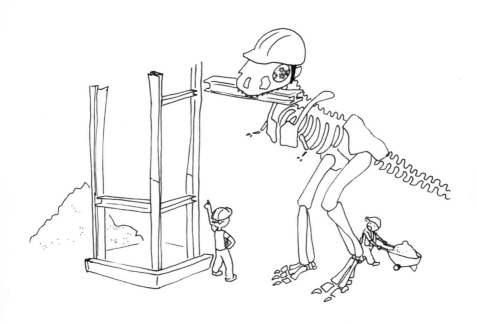

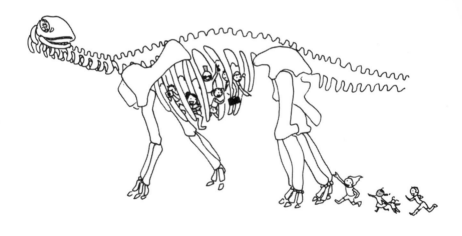

"Apatosaurus, mostly commonly known as Brontosaurus, is your solution to pollution and the rising cost of fuel."

"Triceratops can clear your streets and keep them safe in the snowiest winter months."

The heroes listened, but couldn't believe their ears. Professor B.C. had used Petoskey stones to awaken dozens of other dinosaurs. That was what hid beyond the crowd. Dinosaur after dinosaur, just like in the cave paintings.

What was more, the smartasaurus wanted to personally thank the heroes. None of this would have been possible without them.

"And I have a special gift for my friends Abigail, Andrew, and Zoë—the Heroes A2Z," Professor B.C. said pleasantly. "Please come see what it is."

CHAPTER 9:
STRANDED!

"Look in the sky!" a woman in the crowd shouted. "It's a bird!"

"No, it's a plane!" said someone else.

They were both wrong. Something was flying toward them, but it wasn't a bird or a plane. It wasn't even a caped crusader. Take it from Zoë, she would know.

It was a flock of flying reptiles. *Huge* flying reptiles called pteranodons. Each one of them was big enough to pick up and carry an adult.

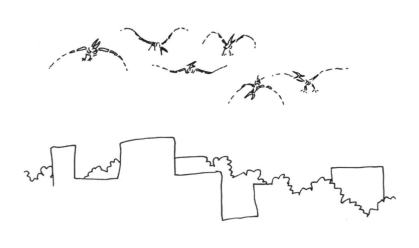

Zoë glanced at Professor B.C. "Deception," she said, and the dinosaur shrugged.

Pteranodons weren't dinosaurs. They both knew that. They were reptiles that had lived at the same time as dinos. Apparently that was close enough for the smartasaurus.

"My friends want to take you for a ride," he told the heroes, and three pteranodons suddenly swooped down low. One snatched Abigail in its bony talons. One caught Andrew. The third grabbed Zoë.

Then up, up, and far away the mighty reptiles soared, carrying the heroes with them.

At first the heroes screamed and kicked.

"Put us down!" Andrew demanded.

"Let go!" ordered Abigail.

"Drop!" Zoë almost said before she remembered that her brother and sister couldn't fly.

The ground was a long way down already. A drop would be deadly. Better to see where the pteranodons took them than to try bungee jumping without a cord.

Where they were taken was South Manitou Island. That was the smaller of two islands near the famous Sleeping Bear Dunes. No one lived there or visited long. It was secluded, quiet, and miles from shore.

As legend tells it, a mother bear and her two cubs had tried to swim across Lake Michigan from Wisconsin. Only the mother bear made it. The cubs became the islands, and the mother became the dunes. She fell asleep on the shore waiting for her children to arrive.

Unlike the mother bear, the heroes weren't given the chance to swim. The pteranodons soared in low and dropped them on the island. Then the reptiles joined their flock and started to circle the island like prison guards making the rounds.

The heroes were trapped. Stranded! Just like in that movie where the guy talked to a soccer ball.

Zoë, of course, refused to give up. She wasn't about to talk to a soccer ball, and she certainly wasn't going to eat any berries, nuts, or wiggly things under rocks. Tea parties with a dinosaur were play enough for her.

She was going to fight. Now.

Up she sped, leading with both fists. *Pow!* The nearest pteranodon didn't know what hit it, nor would it have believed. A kid in a diaper wasn't supposed to pack so much punch.

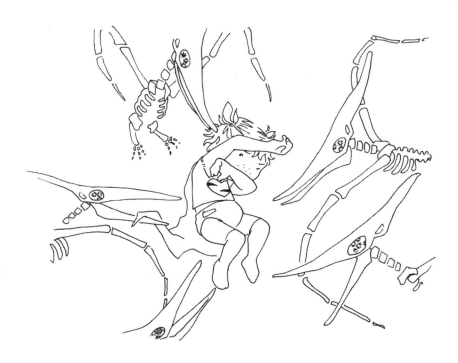

Unfortunately that was all the time she got. One punch and one down. Five more still to go.

The remaining pteranodons dove toward her like hungry gulls fighting over a scrap of bread. They snapped their beaks. They hissed and spat. Soon Zoë's cape was a tattered rag.

She fell like a stone, knocked out cold. The pteranodons had won.

CHAPTER 10:
DISTRACTION ACTION

Thinking fast, Abigail dipped into her duffle bag. She stored all kinds of athletic equipment in there, but the bag never weighed her down. That was a part of her sporting superpower.

Out of it came her trusty catcher's mitt. It was well oiled and soft. In other words, perfect.

"I got it, I got it," she shouted, waving her brother off like an outfielder calling for the ball.

Smack!

Only this wasn't a ball she was catching. It was Zoë's butt!

Zoë came to shortly, and the heroes started to think. They had to escape the island fast, but how? The pteranodons were patrolling the sky.

"They'll see us out on the water," Andrew noted, and Abigail nodded.

"We need something to keep them busy," she said. "Some kind of—"

"Distraction," Zoë chimed in. Better yet, she had the perfect plan. A sneaky, secret plan. It would get them off the island or nothing would.

Andrew was sent to find logs, as many as he could. Zoë didn't explain why she needed them, but Andrew didn't mind. The assignment gave him a chance to use his wheels. That was all that mattered to him.

So he brought Zoë more logs than she could shake a stick at. Though why she would shake a stick at anything made him wonder.

Abigail chopped the logs that Andrew hauled in. A golf club from her duffle bag worked like an axe in her hands. In no time wood chips were flying faster than at a Chomp-a-Thon in Beaverville.

Zoë used the cut logs in two ways. First she tied some of them together to make a raft. Next she carefully carved out three of them with her eye lasers.

"Done," she announced when she finished and stepped back to admire her work. Abigail and Andrew's mouths fell open.

There on the raft stood three wooden statues. An athletic Abigail statue, an accelerating Andrew statue, and a zooming Zoë statue. There was just one problem. The Zoë statue was twice as big as the other two.

"I think you got the sizes mixed up," Andrew muttered, but Abigail quickly jabbed him in the ribs.

"Great job, Zoë," she said. "Now please help me push the raft into the water."

Naturally Zoë did her one better. She took a deep breath and exhaled.

Whoo-oo-oosh! The little raft rapidly glided out onto Lake Michigan.

Then the heroes watched and waited with their fingers crossed. It wouldn't be long before they knew if their plan had worked.

CHAPTER 11:
A DARING ESCAPE

Squawk!
The heroes didn't have to wait long.
Squawk! Squawk!
Nor did they need to keep their fingers crossed. Their plan worked perfectly and fast. As soon as the pteranodons spotted the raft, they shrieked, dove, and attacked.
Squawk!
The raft and its statues didn't stand a chance.

"Hurry!" Abigail cried. "The clock's winding down. We don't have much time."

She meant the raft wouldn't last long. The distraction was working, and the pteranodons were occupied. They were tearing the raft apart. Just think if the heroes had tried to escape that way!

"Start your engine!" she shouted at Andrew. "Make like a speeding bullet," she told Zoë.

Quickly they put the second half of their escape plan into action. Abigail and Andrew would never let Zoë carry them all the way back to the mainland. The distance was over 10 miles, and they weren't babies. They would however, let Zoë *pull* them across the water.

So Andrew and Abigail water-skied their way to freedom. Who ever said that a daring escape couldn't also be fun?

They arrived in Leland 20 minutes later. That was a small town situated on the "pinky" of Michigan. A part of it, called Fishtown, was built right on top of the water. Pretty cool.

Surprised shop owners, tourists, and fishermen gaped as the heroes came to shore. They had seen yachts, charter boats, catamarans, and tugs pull up. Never a trio of water-skiing superheroes. Even cooler.

The heroes paid no attention to the stares. Professor B.C. was up to no good, and Traverse City was still over 20 miles away. There wasn't time to explain or to sign autographs. Michigan needed its heroes.

So Zoë flew, Abigail sprinted, and Andrew skateboarded hard. Together they lasered through Lake Leelanau, sped past Sutton's Bay, and galloped over Greilickville.

Not until they reached Traverse City did they slow down. Then they had to. They couldn't believe their eyes.

CHAPTER 12:
PETOSKEY STONE PRISONERS

Traverse City had changed!

The city the heroes saw now was nothing like the city they had left. All of its people had been turned into slaves.

That explained why Professor B.C. had tried to strand the heroes on South Manitou Island. He had wanted them out of the way. No superhero interference.

As it was, he and his dino army had rounded up the townsfolk and put them to work. Many of them were forced to search endlessly for Petoskey stones along the shore.

Some dug for dinosaur bones while others as-sembled the pieces.

More and more townsfolk arrived in the ribcages of brontosauruses like prisoners in mobile jails. None of them was smiling or happy about reducing pollution now. They were trapped and helpless.

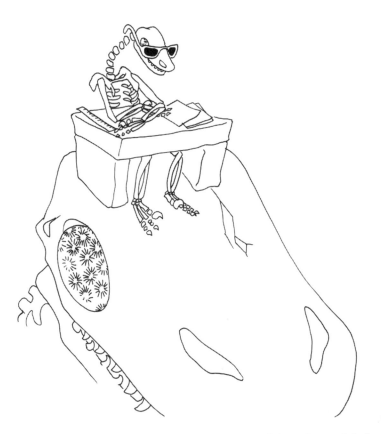

Professor B.C. oversaw everything from high in the air, scowling like a substitute teacher who liked rules more than children. He sat behind a desk that was propped upon a tyrannosaurus's head. How it had gotten there, the heroes could only guess. It was the same desk they had seen yesterday in the underground classroom.

How long ago that seemed! Had it been only a day? So much had happened, and so much had gone wrong.

So much, in fact, that Zoë refused to waste any more time. She flew straight up to the t-rex's toothy snout and pointed a finger in warning.

"Desist!" she bellowed at the top of her lungs. It was her way of saying, "Stop!"

Professor B.C., however, didn't listen or obey. He had already tried to do away with the heroes once. He wasn't afraid to try again.

"Attack!" he howled, smacking a metal ruler on his desk. "Attack!"

An instant later the whole beach started to shake. A battle was about to begin.

CHAPTER 13:
TRIASSIC TIDAL WAVE

Every dinosaur within hearing distance responded to Professor B.C.'s command. First they turned to face the heroes. Then they started to charge.

Stegosaurus sprinted, triceratops trotted, allosaurus ambled, and diplodocus dashed. Every kind of dinosaur came toward the trio performing every kind of run. Together they formed a prehistoric stampede. A Triassic tidal wave. Abigail, Andrew, and Zoë had nowhere to hide.

So they didn't. They couldn't. Hiding and giving up just weren't something the heroes would ever do. That was part of what made them heroes.

"Sound the bell," Abigail growled like a boxer in the ring. She and her siblings were ready for a rumble. Let the battle begin. Ding, ding.

Abigail was so ready, in fact, that she took the dinosaurs by surprise. Maybe you've heard of a preemptive strike. Well, she gave the dinos a pre-emptive *spike.* An overhand serve of her volleyball was all it took.

Thwap!

The dinosaurs leading the charge barely knew what hit them. Abigail's swat smashed into their ranks and sent many of them flying. Their bones scattered like Legos, and the Petoskey stones fell out of their eyes.

Just like that it was one serving zero with Abigail in the lead.

Zoë leaped into action next.

"Demolition!" she shouted, balling up her tiny fists. Then she smacked the ground between her feet and let the dinos have it.

Thoo-oom!

Mighty tremors shook the ground. Sand and stones erupted into the air.

As they went up, the remaining dinosaurs went down. Talk about falling apart! Skeletons just couldn't keep it together during Zoë's earthquake.

Andrew celebrated the quick win with a few victory laps around the beach. But he didn't simply walk or run. Neither was his style. He found the perfect set of wheels for the occasion and made sure the dinosaur bones stayed down.

A steamroller worked. It easily mashed the mixed-up bones down into the sand, back where they belonged.

Naturally Professor B.C. had a backup plan. All cunning supervillains did. It was time for him to unleash his secret weapon.

Before the heroes could nab him, he quickly sent his last Petoskey stone skipping into Lake Michigan. It was a perfect specimen, smooth and oval.

One skip, two skips, three, four—
Clack!

A skeletal hand as long as a picnic table reached out of the water to snatch the stone. Whatever that hand belonged to was bigger than a tyrannosaurus rex. Bigger than *two* t-rexes.

Round two of Abigail's boxing match was about to begin.

CHAPTER 14:
DINOZILLA

Lake Michigan steamed and bubbled like lava spat from an erupting volcano. Angry waves crashed onto the shore.

From the watery depths rose an enormous dinosaur. It was as tall as a semi-truck was long, and looked like a cross between a tyrannosaurus rex and a stegosaurus. The plates on its back were made completely of Petoskey stones. So were its eyes.

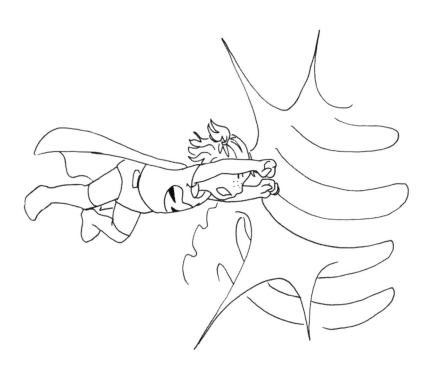

"Dinozilla!" Zoë gasped, perfectly naming the creature. This new dinosaur wasn't just a fossilized skeleton come to life. It was a monster like none she and her siblings had seen before.

In a blur, Zoë sped forward. Her fists cut through the air. Then—

W-h-a-mmm!

She struck Dinozilla and an explosion of sound echoed throughout town. Buildings shook, trees bent, and cars skidded off the streets.

What a wallop! What a punch! It would have leveled any normal dinosaur. But Dinozilla wasn't normal, and the blow hadn't harmed it.

Zoë might as well have been an insect. Dinozilla saw her as something to be squished.

Out swept the dinosaur's tail, snapping at Zoë like a giant whip. Once—*swat!* Twice—*swat!* Three times—*swat!*—it swung. Then disaster struck and little Zoë ran out of luck.

Dinosaur tail and superhero collided with a boom. Zoë was blasted like a homerun ball smacked out of Comerica Park. She didn't just fly high. She didn't only speed. She was sent flying and speeding farther than she had ever thought possible.

Splash!

She flew so far, in fact, that she landed in the Tahquamenon Falls of the Upper Peninsula. They were about 200 miles away from Traverse City!

That left Andrew and Abigail to face Dinozilla alone. Saving Traverse City was up to them now. The rest of the townsfolk had run screaming for their lives.

"You go high," Andrew told his sister.

"And you go low," she replied.

It wasn't much of a plan, they knew, but it was all they had. Maybe two heroes would succeed where one had failed.

"On three," Abigail said, getting ready to run.

But instead of the expected countdown, Andrew shoved his sister in the back, jumped onto the closest thing with wheels, and shouted.

"Three!" Forget one and two. It was time to attack.

CHAPTER 15:
DINOSAUR BREATH

Abigail attacked first, but Andrew wasn't far behind. She slammed down her pole and vaulted into the air. He cranked the brakes on the stroller and let his momentum do the rest. Both of them shot forward like missiles.

Who said all superheroes couldn't fly?

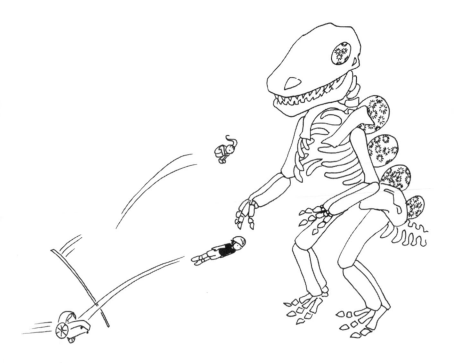

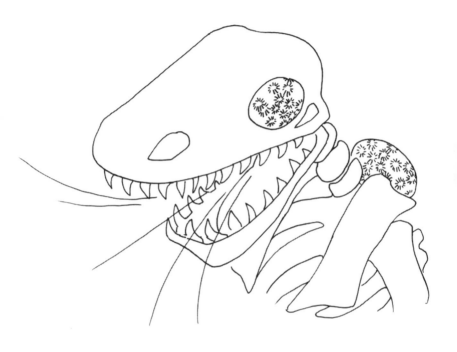

Dinozilla, that was who. The heroes found that out the hard way. The very hard, bony way.

First Abigail and then Andrew crashed into the dinosaur. Thump one, *ouch!* Thump two, *oof!* That was as close as they got.

But they could get farther. Farther away, that was. Dinozilla saw to that. As the heroes fell, the monster reared back as if getting ready to sneeze and then let out a terrible roar.

GRRR-ROWR!

93

The dinosaur's roar was a hurricane of bad breath and noise. When it struck, the twins couldn't decide whether to cover their noses or their ears. All of their senses were suffering.

The gust sent them spinning helplessly backward. Over the beach, the road, and the parking lot full of cars. Straight toward downtown Traverse City.

Then, like Zoë, they landed with a splash. *Splish!* Right in Boardman River.

Abigail popped to the surface first, coughing and spitting out water. But she wasn't complaining. Not in the least. After being blasted by Dinozilla's breath, she had needed and wanted a bath.

Her brother surfaced next to her, and she immediately grabbed his collar.

"Make like a fish," she said. "We don't have much time."

Andrew grunted and started kicking his feet. He wasn't nearly as good a swimmer as Abigail. No one was.

"Know any fish that have wheels?" he grumbled.

They barely reached the dock before Dinozilla
was on top of them again. Abigail scrambled up first
and then offered a hand to her brother. As Andrew
hauled himself out of the water, Dinozilla arrived.

Grr-rowr! The monster roared again.

But this time the dinosaur wasn't trying to blast
the twins. Its head was high. Its roar was a roar of
victory, not battle.

It raised one of its huge feet, and an icy shadow
fell over the heroes. Dinozilla was going to flatten
them.

CHAPTER 16:
SLURP AND SPLURT

Back at the Tahquamenon Falls, Zoë was in the water and down but not out. She was so down and deep, in fact, that swimming wasn't her best option. Drinking was.

Why swim to the surface, she decided, when she could bring the surface to her.

Slu-r-r-r-p!

And so she drank and drank and slurped and slurped until she couldn't hold any more. But she didn't swallow. She wasn't thirsty. She had a sneak attack planned for Dinozilla.

Flying with a superhero-sized mouthful of water wasn't easy. Zoë had to breathe through her nose all the way back to Traverse City, and hope like crazy that she didn't sneeze.

Had that happened, she was ready with the perfect word: "Disaster."

The flight could have been worse, she knew. At least no seagulls had tried to land on her head.

When Zoë reached town, Dinozilla was easy to spot. So was its deadly plan. The dinosaur hulked on the edge of Boardman River, ready to crush something beneath its massive foot.

Make that *two* somethings, Zoë realized. Her brother and sister. Abigail and Andrew hadn't defeated Dinozilla either. They were in terrible danger.

Splurt!

Thinking fast, she slapped her cheeks with the palms of her hands, and the water burst from her mouth. It slammed Dinozilla square in the face, knocking the monster off balance. After that, there was nowhere for it to go but down.

Sploo-oo-oosh!

Dinozilla toppled onto its side and fell over into the river. Waves battered the nearby dock. Water erupted into the air.

Abigail screamed and Andrew howled, but both of them went with the water. They flapped their arms and kicked their feet. Were they supposed to be fish or birds?

Luckily Zoë swooped in and caught them before they started to fall. She really wanted to pick another fight with Dinozilla, but her siblings were more important.

Besides, the giant dinosaur had already beaten her once. Then it had done the same to her siblings. Zoë was smart enough to known when to escape and regroup. Even superheroes had their limits.

So she didn't stick around for Dinozilla to get up. She decided that she and her siblings had somewhere else to be.

"Where are we going?" Abigail asked.

"Turn around!" demanded Andrew.

But the two of them were helpless again, this time under Zoë's control. She clutched them by their belt loops and dragged them south without a word.

Past the airport and almost to the edge of town, Zoë finally landed in a small parking lot. Then she nodded at the building ahead of them.

"Doggies," she said.

They were standing outside the Cherryland Humane Society. Why?

CHAPTER 17:
DEPUTY DOGS

Andrew and Abigail shrugged at each other. Neither could guess what their little sister was up to this time.

Meanwhile, Zoë was busy getting up to it. She was already inside the building and doing what no one expected. She was letting all of the puppies and dogs in the Cherryland Humane Society go free!

"Deputies!" she smiled at the confused employee who came running. Her explanation didn't help.

"I think I get it," Abigail said, finally understanding. She could translate Zoë-speak as well as anyone. "Zoë is looking for backup. Pretend she's a sheriff. The dogs will be her deputies."

That was exactly it. Heroes A²Z wasn't a police force, but it was a force to be reckoned with. Add a few dozen yapping, yipping deputies, and the heroes might be able to take on Dinozilla.

Naturally Zoë led the charge. She was the sheriff of this furry bunch.

"Dinner!" she bellowed, causing quite the excitement. She might as well have asked, "Who wants to go outside?" Every dog in the building started to dance.

And why not? They knew what was coming. A delicious game of dine-and-go-seek. Think canine Thanksgiving and Easter rolled into one.

The heroes waited on the roof like warriors. Zoë stood in the middle with Abigail on her right and Andrew to her left. Next to them stretched a row of dogs and puppies that reached all the way to the corners of the building.

Not one of them moved, not human or canine. They hardly even breathed. They waited in silence for Dinozilla to arrive.

Which didn't take long. The gigantic dinosaur's long legs carried it rapidly across Traverse City. Nothing in its path slowed it down. Not buildings, traffic lights, telephone wires, or stop signs.

Stopping it was the heroes' responsibility.

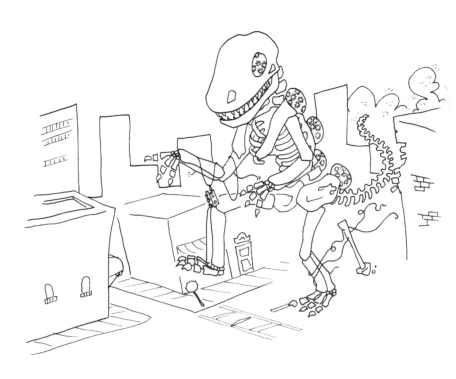

CHAPTER 18:
GIVE A DOG A BONE

Dinozilla stormed into the parking lot of the Cherryland Humane Society like a bully looking for a fight. Cracks split the asphalt beneath its heavy feet. Vibrations ran all the way up to the heroes on the roof.

"It looks mad," Andrew said warily.

"Must have a bone to pick with us," Abigail agreed, smirking. Think of it, a skeleton with a bone to pick. Genius! Maybe comedy was Abigail's superpower, not athletics.

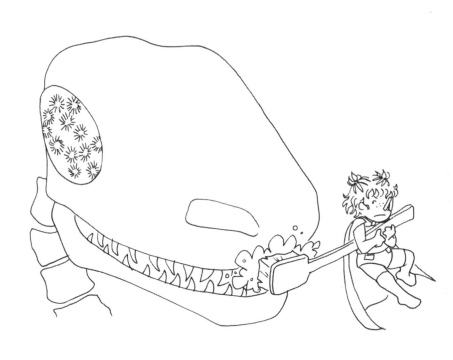

Either way, Dinozilla didn't laugh. But it did take a deep breath as if it might. It reared back its head and even opened its mouth. Then it roared straight into the faces of the heroes and almost blew them off the roof.

GRRR-ROWR!

Pee-yew! Stinky breath! Dinozilla's reek was worse than it's roar. Obviously dinosaurs had died out *way* before toothbrushes and mouthwash had been invented.

"*S*-smells like your duffel bag," Andrew gasped.

"More like your … *cough* … rollerblades," wheezed Abigail.

Just like that, it was punch/counter-punch. The twins went at it head-to-head. Or better yet, in a battle of smells, they went at it nose-to-nose.

When they ran out of insults for each other, they rounded on Zoë. She wore a diaper. Perfect target!

"Smells as bad as Zoë's d—," they started together.

But Zoë cut them off with a raised finger and dark look. "Don't," was all she said, and everyone within hearing distance quickly closed their mouths.

Everyone including the dogs on the roof. They snapped their jaws shut and bared their teeth. Dinozilla had made some noise. Now it was their turn.

Like canine carolers at Christmastime, the dogs raised their voices together. Great Danes growled, shepherds snarled, beagles barked, and malamutes did not stay mute. Big and small, every dog lent its voice to the woofing choir.

GRR-ROWLLL!

The noise was deafening and the result spectacular. So much more so than Dinozilla's roar. Even the heroes had to cover their ears.

As for Dinozilla, it shrank back, looking suddenly small. Fear shone in its Petoskey-stone eyes.

"You're in for it, bonehead!" Abigail teased.

"Doghouse," Zoë nodded, meaning that was where Dinozilla was headed. For anyone but a dog, being sent to the doghouse was as bad as a grounding.

The dogs, however, weren't finished yet. They had Dinozilla down but not out. One brave yellow lab wearing a red bandana around its neck led the charge. Belting out a bark, it leaped courageously from the rooftop. The rest of the pack immediately followed.

For a heroic moment, the dogs were flying. They were superheroes, too! Watch out, Krypto. Move over, Underdog. Here come Heroes Arf to Tzu.

Their landing was impressive, too, and also rather loud. Jaws snapped and teeth clacked. Dinner had finally been served. Chomp!

Forget about crime. These dogs had more on their plates, or more in their bowls to be precise. Because when it came to prehistoric dinosaurs, they took a bite out of time.

And bones! They took a bite out of bones. Leg bones, arm bones, and anklebones, too. Any kind they could fit into their mouths.

Hapless Dinozilla didn't stand a chance. Soon the monster was in pieces again, exactly the way it belonged.

In fact, make that the way and *where* it belonged. Because the dogs didn't just bite. They did what every dog does with a good bone. They scampered out of sight and buried Dinozilla's bones all over town.

Now only one dinosaur remained standing. Professor B.C.

CHAPTER 19:
ADOPTION DAY

Abigail raced her siblings back to the beach. Just because they had defeated Dinozilla didn't mean they could slow down. Professor B.C. was still at large and had to be stopped. He could build another army of dino-skeletons if the heroes didn't hurry.

"He isn't by the volleyball nets," Abigail announced, the first to arrive.

"He's gone," Andrew shrugged.

"Disappeared," Zoë agreed.

"Where?" Andrew muttered, kicking the sand at his feet. "Where did he go?"

Abigail shared her brother's frustration. Professor B.C. could be anywhere, and the heroes didn't have a clue. What good was it being superheroes if they couldn't catch the bad guys?

"He's probably looking for more Petoskey stones," she said. "More stones mean more—"

She didn't finish. Suddenly Zoë leaped up and started pointing at her nose. With the other hand, she pointed at Abigail.

"Ding, ding!" she exclaimed. "Ding, ding!"

"She means you hit it on the nose," Andrew explained quickly. "Something you said was right."

Abigail shrugged. "Petoskey stones?" she wondered, but didn't wonder long.

"Destination!" Zoë beamed, now pointing at her sister with both hands.

"Petoskey sto—*oh!*" Abigail exclaimed. "You mean Petoskey the city. Petoskey, Michigan."

Petoskey, Michigan exactly. Where better to look for Petoskey stones than a place named after them? Better still, the town was only about an hour's drive away. Not bad for the heroes. They had gone farther than that to stop villains before, and could make it in half the time.

So Andrew found the first thing he could wheel nearby, which turned out to be the paddleboat he had used to tow his sisters earlier.

"All aboard!" he shouted. Next stop, Petoskey, Michigan. They would get their in record time. But not as the car cruises or the crow flies. They would do it as the salmon swims—across Lake Michigan.

Professor B.C. wasn't hard to spot. He was on the beach in Petoskey, gathering stones in a bucket. Sure, he was wearing a disguise, but it wasn't very good. His tail stuck out of the back of his swimming trunks!

"Detention," Zoë told Professor B.C., snatching the bucket out of his hand.

"That's right," Abigail said. "You won't be needing any more Petoskey stones."

"Not unless the police put you to work polishing them in jail," Andrew added, which wasn't a bad guess.

The police did put Professor B.C. in jail, but not to polish stones. He was a teacher, so they put him to work grading homework. Enough to keep him busy until graduation—in year 2099!

As for the canine heroes from the Cherryland Humane Society, they all found new homes. Every dog and puppy was adopted that very afternoon. Thanks in part to Zoë for advertising. Thanks mostly to the Humane Society for caring.

The heroes, unfortunately, couldn't adopt a pet that day. Their lives were too full of danger. Villains and bad guys could show up in the least likely places and at the least likely times. They could even spoil an egg hunt in …

Book #5:
Easter Egg Haunt

www.heroesa2z.com

Visit the Website

realheroesread.com

Meet Authors Charlie & David
Read Sample Chapters
See Fan Artwork
Join the Free Fan Club
Invite Charlie & David to Your School
Lots More!

Visit
www.heroesa2z.com
for the latest news

Also by David Anthony and Charles David

Monsters. Magic. Mystery.

#1: Cauldron Cooker's Night
#2: Skull in the Birdcage
#3: Early Winter's Orb
#4: Voyage to Silvermight
#5: Trek Through Tangleroot
#6: Hunt for Hollowdeep
#7: The Ninespire Experiment
#8: Aware of the Wolf

Visit
www.knightscares.com
to learn more

#1: Cauldron Cooker's Night

#2: Skull in the Birdcage

#3: Early Winter's Orb

#4: Voyage to Silvermight
The Dragonbane Horn Book One

#5: Trek Through Tanglewood
The Dragonbane Horn Book Two

#6: Hunt for Hollowdeep
The Dragonbane Horn Book Three

#7: The Ninespire Experiment

#8: Aware of the Wolf

127

About the Illustrator
Lys Blakeslee

Lys graduated from Grand Valley State University in Michigan where she pursued a degree in Illustration.

She has always loved to read, and devoted much of her childhood to devouring piles of books from the library.

She spends her summers in Wyoming, MI with her wonderful parents, three younger brothers, two happy cats, and two noisy parakeets.

Broccoli, spinach and ice cream are a few of her favorite foods.

Thank you, Lys!